UNITED
STATES OF
AMERICA

SOUTH
KOREA

SOYUNG'S JOURNEY

SOYUNG, AS AN INFANT IN SOUTH KOREA, WITH HER PARENTS

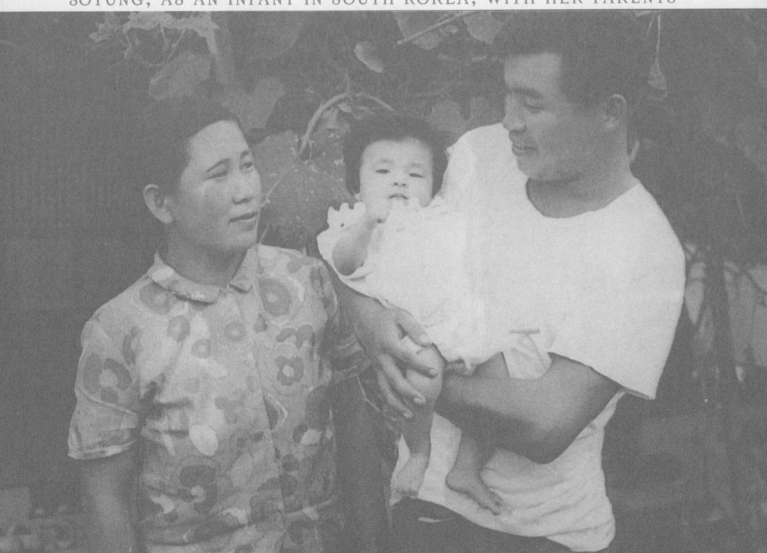

A Place To Grow

BY SOYUNG PAK

ILLUSTRATED BY MARCELINO TRUONG

ARTHUR A. LEVINE BOOKS
AN IMPRINT OF SCHOLASTIC PRESS

The earth is soft.

The sun still shimmers wet from its long

snowy winter nap.

This is the seed time. This is the growing time.

When seeds flying in the wind find their gardens to grow in

and finally land.

My father knows all about this.

He knows all about flying.

He flew a long way to grow into our family.

Over streets and highways and farms,

over melon gardens and rivers and mountains,

even an ocean to grow into a family.

"All seeds travel," my dad says.

"Some seeds just hop from where they were born.

Others catch the winds and fly far, far away."

If you ask him why, my father will tell you a seed needs land to grow.

"But there is land everywhere," I say

as we walk careful steps, measuring exactly where our garden will be.

My father stops, digs through the grass,

and sifts through the dark black dirt with his hands.

"Not good land," he says.

"Good land is warm and safe, like a cozy home.

It protects the seed and helps it to grow.

"But sometimes land is cold and rocky.

Instead of offering shelter, it surrounds the seed

with the sharp edges of stones.

That is what happens when there are too many guns

and not enough love.

A place like that is no place to grow a flower."

"So the seed flew with the wind?" I ask.

"So it flew with the wind," he says.

If you ask him why, he will tell you a seed needs sun to grow.

"But the sun shines on everything," I say.

It shines too much, I think, as I feel it hot on my neck,

making me all sticky and wet.

My father stops weeding to give me his hat.

It flops over my eyes and onto my nose.

It smells like dandelion and shampoo

and makes my neck feel shaded and cool.

"It doesn't shine on everything," he says.

"The sun doesn't shine where shadows fall.

And sometimes a seed falls in the gloomy shade.

It gets left in the dark with no sun to light the way.

That is what it is like when there are dreams but not enough hope.

A place like that is no place to grow a flower."

"So the seed flew with the wind?" I ask.

"It flew with the wind," he says.

If you ask him why, my father will tell
you that a seed needs rain to grow.
Even as it brings dark skies and chases us
inside, my father tells me this.

At the window, I see the raindrops slide
down the misty glass, sketching crooked
bars. I see the rain beat down against the
growing plants. I see the garden bend
and bow and shake toward the wet and
muddy ground.

"A seed needs rain to grow.

The rain that fell on our seed came only now and then,

and sometimes not at all.

Instead of overflowing lakes and ponds,

the dryness withered all the plants.

That is what it is like when there are too many workers

and not enough work.

A place like that is no place to grow a flower."

"So the seed flew with the wind?" I ask.

"Yes, we flew with the wind," he says.

"We flew with the wind."

Now there is magic in my father's garden.

Colors sprout like swelling balloons.

There are tomatoes and peppers in it to

help me grow and flowers that open

for the sun in the afternoon.

At night, it glistens

and glows along with the stars

and the moon.

Together my father and I listen to the wind

rustling through these growing plants.

We sit under the sun.

We feel the soft dirt under our feet.

We know that the rain will come.

"Will I fly with the wind?" I ask.

"Maybe," he says. "Or maybe you'll just take a hop."

"Either way," he says,

"we'll always be family.

We'll always be close."

And if you ask him why, my father will tell

what his father told him.

"Even if you fly across the tallest mountains,

the longest roads, and the widest seas,

there will always be a garden in my heart for you."

Even if I fly across the tallest mountains,

the longest roads, and the widest seas,

there will always be a garden

in his heart for me.

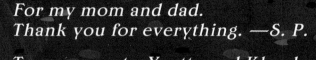

For my mom and dad.
Thank you for everything. —*S. P.*

To my parents, Yvette and Khanh.
—M. T.

Text copyright © 2002 by Soyung Pak • Illustrations copyright © 2002 by Marcelino Truong • All rights reserved.
Published by Scholastic Press, a division of Scholastic Inc., *Publishers since 1920.* SCHOLASTIC, SCHOLASTIC PRESS, and the
LANTERN LOGO are trademarks and/or registered trademarks of Scholastic Inc. • No part of this publication may be repro-
duced, or stored in a retrieval system, or transmitted in any form or by any means, electronic, mechanical, photocopy-
ing, recording, or otherwise, without written permission of the publisher. • For information regarding permission, write
to Scholastic Inc., Attention: Permissions Department, 557 Broadway, New York, NY 10012. • LIBRARY OF CONGRESS CAT-
ALOGING-IN-PUBLICATION DATA • Pak, Soyung. A Place to Grow / by Soyung Pak ; illustrated by Marcelino Truong p.   cm.
Summary: As a father tells his daughter what a seed needs to flourish, he also explains the reasons he emigrated to a
new homeland. • ISBN 0-439-13015-8 • [1. Fathers and daughters—Fiction. 2. Emigration and immigration—Fiction. 3.
Gardening—Fiction.] I. Truong, Marcelino, ill. II. Title. PZ7.P173 P1 2002   [E]—dc21 • 00-053494 •
10 9 8 7 6 5 4 3 2 1   02 03 04 05 06 • Printed in Mexico • 49 • First edition, September 2002 • Text set in 17-point
Edwardian Medium • The artwork was created using China ink with gouache paint • Book design by Marijka Kostiw

MARCELINO, AGED 5 IN VIETNAM, IN FRONT OF HIS FATHER

ENGLAND

VIETNAM

MARCELINO'S JOURNEY